SHORT STORIES

YOGENDRA NIKALE

written by yogendra nikale
car wash [short video script]
song : la vi en rose

the boy is sleeping and next to him there is a table placed. his father enters the frame and keeps a glass of milk and wakes him and exits the frame.

the boy gets up and watches and wears his glasses, and takes the milk glass, and the boys asks his father in sign where are you going the father has bucket in his hand and signs him that i going for the car wash come.

the boy signs no and points the school bag hanged on a wall behind his father. as he is going to colledge.

the boy takes his bycycle and bog on his back heads towards college.

the boy was riding his bycle on the way and a open gypsy comes from back in a high speed and gives him a jerk kind of a bully thing and he stops and the car leaves. the girl he likes and her friends are in that car.

as they go boy starts pedling again and heads towards the college.

he reaches and he watches that the car car is parked and he enters the college.

he stalks the girl everywhere in the college. but he never talks.

because she hangs out with the cool kids in the college.

he watches her in the lecture but she never notices.

he stalks her in the library.

he watches her in the canteen.

he makes a sketch of her when she in the library.

and duringg the music session, the girl is playing the trumpet and he has her sketch in his hand and he starts dreaming of her and they are ball dancing in the classroom. and everyone are happy watching them together and sparklers are coming from above. a beautiful scene.

the boy next to him snatches his book of sketch and passes to next, even she watches the sketch but there comes the evil boy he gets angry watching her sketch and slaps the boy and his glasses fly and broke. everryone just stares and even the girl.
the boy runs away from that classroom.
next day when his father wakes him up. the boy drinks the milk and sign his father where to
the fathers sign him car wash and you go to college.
the boy sign no college, im also gonna do car wash.
his father gives a tense look but says nothing.
in college the girl is searching the boy
they boy is doing car wash now.
the boy's father raises up a sign board of car was on the street and next to him his son raises board of 60rs only.
random car wash scenes and the boy has beard now.
once he was eating burger on the street and his father was counting the money and he watches him, he feels very bad for him.
the evil boy in his jeepsy makes the girl drunk at night in some parking of a building. and he tries to take advantage of her. tries to touch her, tries to kiss her but she denies, so he slaps her, removes her from the car and leaves her there and goes away
the boy is washing car on the street and the girl is walking.
the girl watches him and recognizes him.
they stare each other for 2 seconds
she signs hi.
he sign hi back.
she signs nice mustache
the boy signs why are you crying.
the girl nods nothing and gives him his glasses, she fixed it. as he takes the evil boy comes and gets out of his car.
the girl comes behind the boy.

the evil boy signs her to get in the car.
she looks at the car wash boy and says no.
the evil comes to grab her, but the boy punches him and grabs a mob to beat him. the evil boy falls down.
he watches them and gets in the car and goes.
they both hug and there comes his father and he snatches the mob from the boy's hand, the boy looks ashamed, and father gives him his college bag.
the boy gets shocked and the father smiles.
next day the boy and the girl both went to college in his bycycle, they both ar together in the library, i canteen and even in classroom they sit next to each other.
cut to
the father raising the sign board of car wash. the boy and the girl enter in his bycycle. the boy raise the sign of 60 rs only. and the girl raises the sign of i love him
the end.

Contents

CHAPTER ONE

written by yogendra nikale
deja vu [short film script]
song
scene 1
there is a desk, and over the desk there is a gift box and a lamp a 10 year old boy enters the frame turns the lamps light on and watches the gift. he lifts the gift it says happy birthday danny my loving son.
danny starts unpacking. its a fairytale. the boy gets very happy after watching it. he opens the book and starts reading. random shots of turning pages and at the end the he reads the prince and the princes lives happily ever after.

he shuts tthe book and he sits dreaming and the camera gets zoom in his eye. he gets a long shot vision of a girl coming outside the house.
he wakes up from the dream and gets up. he opens his closet and tkes the paint out and he starts painting.
alarm on desk close up shot and pan to the boy is sleeping his head on the desk and the painting of the house and the girl.
scene 2
the father and the son is behind the curtuns. the father is yelling at him and gives him the report card [contour shot] the son comes to his desk in his room and sits in his chair.

he wipes his tears and watches the report card. the report card says its zero and the zero morphss into the depth of the well and zoom out and he gets a vision of the well. the boy comes out of his vision and throws away the report card and starts painting.

the camera on watch and time lapse. camera pan to the boy. and he is done with the painting of well and he keeps it in a file.

scene 3

few years later.

dany is all grown up and he keeps his books in his bag and suddenly the fairy tale fells from the book shelf in his desk he smile looking at it and keeps the book back.

he watches himself in the mirror and he gets a vision that backsideof a boy with blonde hair and a girls hand is touching his hair. then he comes out of his vision. hegoes down the mirror and as he comes up he has blonde hair he looks the mirror turns towards his guitar and exits.

scene 4

in evening dany walking on the street with his guitar on his back. police is chsing a burglar on the street and they bump into him anh falls down he gets up and sit on the foot path to checks his guitar and start fixing . he watches to his left a car is coming and the car headlight mormphs into lamp in the hand of horse cart.

and as he comes out of the vision the car driver throws pop corn on him and yell, dany runs away from that spot.

scene 5

dany comes home, he gets all his paints together and starts painting

colour effect in bowl of water cinematic effect.

he paints the horse cart man and he keeps next to his guitar and feels bad for his broken guitar and suddenly he gets a vision of a train entering the tunnel.

timme lapse od night till day and he is till painting.

scene 6

dany is teaching guitar to small children in the a studio. and a girls hand comes on the dany's shoulder and then it disapears. he feels something and he watches here and there aand then his eyes stops on the wall poster saying follow your dream and he gets another vision of a sighn board board saying dream land and pointing the direction to the right in a unknown place.

one of the student comes near him and wakes him from this vision and he continues his class again.

scene 7

dany enters the coffe shop and sits on the chair and he shows a sign of 1 coffee to the the counter and one coffee comes on his table by the waiter, dany thanks him and waiter exits as he was about to take a sip of the coffee he looks at girl toward his right table. and he gets a vision.

the vision of a girl with a hanging earing playing with a puppy . as he comes out of the vision the girl gives a sign of punching him what are you staring about.

he gets very anoyed of his visions, keeps money on the table and exits.

scene 8

as dany enters his room he watches a gift on his table, saying happy birthday son. he exitingly opens. its a holidaay ticket to goa. he removes his colours and start painting. and goes to sleep as he goes to sleep the sealing fan turns into a moon.

he gets anoyed and takes his bedsheet on his face

scene 9

dany getting ready for his vacation timlapse, he gets cleaned, wear clothes and fills bag, he comes near the table

for the ticket, he watches his last night painting, [not shown to the audience] puts itt in a file and takes the file with him.
scene 10
dany catches his train and he sits and there is a very sweet 10 year old girl sitting in front of him. he smiles wwatching her.
shots of train travel
he watches outside and suddenly he watches the train is entering the tunnel and he had the same vision and he had painted it. he checks the file and it is same. he gets shocked. the girls signs what happened. he smiles and signs nothing.
scene 11
he reaches his destination, and he hires a pilot towards his hotel but in between he watches the dreamland sign. he asks his pilot to stop and he gets up and compares the sign from the painting and the real view. he decides to follow the dreamland sign.
he takes a long walk and the sunset time lapse.
scene 12
dany walks and he watches a horse man coming.
as he comes near he takes the in front of the dany to see his face sames as vision. and he says to get in the cart.
wheel shots
horse foot shots
dany watching the painting shots
and the road shots.
the horse cart stops and dany gets up he watches there is a open grass in front of him and as he looks back the horse cart has also disapeared.
he comes in the grass and looks up the same moon and he smiles. and sleeps
sunrise timelapse
scene 13

dany wakes up and he watches all flowers around him, he starts walking.
he watches the same well from the vision. he walks furthure
he watches the girl from the vision coming out of the house.
the girl playing with the puppy and the hanging earing. exactly like the vision.
the girl notices him and comes towards him.
she touches his hair like the vision.
he shows her the painting, watching it she hugs and camera pan to the painting the girl is hugging. the page flews away and the other page says the end.

CHAPTER TWO

written by yogendra nikale
car wash [short video script]
song : la vi en rose
the boy is sleeping and next to him there is a table placed. his father enters the frame and keeps a glass of milk and wakes him and exits the frame.
the boy gets up and watches and wears his glasses, and takes the milk glass, and the boys asks his father in sign where are you going
the father has bucket in his hand and signs him that i going for the car wash come.
the boy signs no and points the school bag hanged on a wall behind his father. as he is going to colledge.
the boy takes his bycycle and bog on his back heads towards college.
the boy was riding his bycle on the way and a open gypsy comes from back in a high speed and gives him a jerk kind of a bully thing and he stops and the car leaves. the girl he likes and her friends are in that car.
as they go boy starts pedling again and heads towards the college.
he reaches and he watches that the car car is parked and he enters the college.
he stalks the girl everywhere in the college. but he never

talks. because she hangs out with the cool kids in the college.
he watches her in the lecture but she never notices.
he stalks her in the library.
he watches her in the canteen.
he makes a sketch of her when she in the library.
and duringg the music session, the girl is playing the trumpet and he has her sketch in his hand and he starts dreaming of her and they are ball dancing in the classroom. and everyone are happy watching them together and sparklers are coming from above. a beautiful scene.
the boy next to him snatches his book of sketch and passes to next, even she watches the sketch but there comes the evil boy he gets angry watching her sketch and slaps the boy and his glasses fly and broke. everryone just stares and even the girl.
the boy runs away from that classroom.
next day when his father wakes him up. the boy drinks the milk and sign his father where to
the fathers sign him car wash and you go to college.
the boy sign no college, im also gonna do car wash.
his father gives a tense look but says nothing.
in college the girl is searching the boy
they boy is doing car wash now.
the boy's father raises up a sign board of car was on the street and next to him his son raises board of 60rs only.
random car wash scenes and the boy has beard now.
once he was eating burger on the street and his father was counting the money and he watches him, he feels very bad for him.
the evil boy in his jeepsy makes the girl drunk at night in some parking of a building. and he tries to take advantage of her. tries to touch her, tries to kiss her but she denies, so

he slaps her, removes her from the car and leaves her there and goes away
the boy is washing car on the street and the girl is walking.
the girl watches him and recognizes him.
they stare each other for 2 seconds
she signs hi.
he sign hi back.
she signs nice mustache
the boy signs why are you crying.
the girl nods nothing and gives him his glasses, she fixed it.
as he takes the evil boy comes and gets out of his car.
the girl comes behind the boy.
the evil boy signs her to get in the car.
she looks at the car wash boy and says no.
the evil comes to grab her, but the boy punches him and grabs a mob to beat him. the evil boy falls down.
he watches them and gets in the car and goes.
they both hug and there comes his father and he snatches the mob from the boy's hand, the boy looks ashamed, and father gives him his college bag.
the boy gets shocked and the father smiles.
next day the boy and the girl both went to college in his bycycle, they both ar together in the library, i canteen and even in classroom they sit next to each other.
cut to
the father raising the sign board of car wash. the boy and the girl enter in his bycycle. the boy raise the sign of 60 rs only. and the girl raises the sign of i love him
the end.

CHAPTER THREE

written by : yogendra nikale
tittle : glimpse [script]
scene : 1
shot 1 : dutch angle shot zoom in and blank effect
female model posing in front of the camera and behind her there is a crome and the environment is completelty a photoshoot and the camera flashlight while taking pictures in different costumes and props

shot 2 : dutch angle shot zoom out.
the camera is behind the looser and he is taking pictures of the model

shot 3 : ducth angle shot zoom in.
looser taking pictures side view

shot 4 : looser point of view shot from camera
looser taking picturc osf thhc modcl and suddenly the camera stops working.

shot 5 : looser checking the camera side view and fixing the batery .

shot 6 : ots of the looser or the close up shot of the model.
model : what happened, why did you stopped the glimpse.

shot 7 : looser mid shot
looser : the camera just stopped working.
model : check the battery, the charging must have went off.

looser : i have checked the battery, still the camera is not working.
model : can you fix it today.
looser : i may fix it mbut not today. it might take day or 2.
model : do you have any idea how important this shoot is for me.
the looser listening in guilt shot.
looser : as soon as i fix it we will reshoot again.
model : you have wasted my enough time. i never should have. im out of this sheat hole, and return me my money. [walks near the door]
looser nods yes and looks down.
model near the door : everyone where right about you, you are a fuckin looser. and you will always be.
looser looking at her in guilt.
cut to
scene 2
looser walking long shot
on the left side he watches shops and one shop says camera only for you and he enters the shop.
the shop is very spooky and dark and looser is checking all the stuff from the shop and its all spooky and devil related stuff and suddenly a scary man in a black coat and black hat "how can i help you boy"
looser : i dont want to buy anything, i just want to fix my camera .
the scary man : i dont repair stuff i repair lives.
looser : what do you mean.
scary man : i mean i dont reapair camera, i only sell them. if you want to buy, you are at a right place. tell me which one do you want. [zoom on scary man shot]
looser : i told you i dont want to buy i dont want to buy. i

dont have money.
scary man : atleast you take a look around.
looser : i saw nothing is useful for me.
scary man : wait i have the perfect thing for you. [he takes the vintage camera and shows him] i call it the purifffier. this is for only 15 silver coins.
looser : didnt you hear what i said. i dont have money, and this camera looks older than my grandfather.
scary man : ok 7 silver coins.
looser : its not uselfull for me at all, its very old and i dont even know how to use it.
scary man : [takes the camera in hand and demonstrates] you just have to turn it and click it, and give me only one coin. you have it in your pocket i can smell it from here.
looser : shows a 1 bug coin and says this coin. are you sure.
scary man : yes yes, you can have the camera, thats all you have to give [greddily]
looser : alright, looks like a good deal to me. [tosses the coin to the scary man]
scary man : ohh the silver coin, youu know how much i love you. [looser watches it and picks up the camera and turns the roll of the camera and was about to click the scary man. the scary man gets scared and he stopss] wait wait wait. dont wastc that roll use it very carefully.
the looser stares at him a second and leaves the shop and evil smile of the scaryman.
scene 3
looser watching the camera and walking on the street and suddenly a friend bumps into him and looser says " whatch where you going "
friend : looser you, what are you doing with that old camera. no actually its perfect you deserve such old crap. and look what i deserve. [shows him his new watch] its

from london limited edition, cost equals to you and your ansisters have ever spended. [looser watching in shame] come on take a picture and frame it in your house, this will remind you can never afford such stuff.
looser hesitatingly takes the camera and places near his eye to look through the camera and take the picture
the watch picture is taken from the camera point of view shot.
friend : now get lost, and dont forget you are poor.
as they walk a little further on different dirrects the friend yells " hey what the fuck have you done my watch is ticking backwards. looser looks back once and continues walking.
scene 4
looser walking down the street and watching a girl passes by and a friend comes suddenly in his car and says ‘ hey looser what are you looking at, no girl belongs to you, your a begger, they need guys like us rich and fancy cars. looser watching the friend in shame
friend 2 : whats that your grandmother gave it to you, take a picture this will remind you money talks and bull sheat walks.
looser takes the picture from his camera [camera point of view shot]
and as he takes down the camera from his eyes the friend’s dick is under the car tyre and he is yelling ’what the fuck is happening, how did i get here. someone get me out of here. looser help me help me looser, [looser exits in shock] looser you piece of sheat help me [yelling loudly]
scene 5
looser rushes back towards the shop where he took the camera but he couldnt, but the shop was closed and there were burned marks outside.
looser asks the next shopkeer,, what happened to this

shope.

shopkeeper : this shop is closed from past 50 years there was a suddrn fire the greedy shopkeeper died in it.

looser : but today i bought this camera from this shop, how is this possible.

shopkeeper : from this shop, sounds interesting, maybe you can tell this story to a doctor or a mental institution. they might help you.

looser : but listen to me.

shopkeeper : just shut it, now hit the road boy, we have work to do.

looser watches him and passes by the shop watching it.

scene 5

looser long walk and the camera is upside down and it turn back to normal

looser walk from side view.

looser watches a guy is drinking beer and girl next his is smoking in the street and he takes the picture and the beard is on the girl and the girls red hair is on the boy and they started yelling what is this happening.

looser walks and smiles

scene 6

looser walks towards a tea stall, the tea stall guy is giving tea to the people and taking money and he is very rude with the people and starts making tea in a big barel where his sweat is dropping in the tea. and looser watches it.

looser takes the picture and as lower downs the camera the tea stall guy puts the hot tea from the tea pot on his head and he ia smiling.

looser exits that place.

scene 7

looser walks further and he watches a shopkeer is counting money in his shop and outside his shop there is small girl

begging for money and he is neglecting her.
loser takes the picture and the shopkeeper starts blowing money with a smile and all the begger are gathered and starts taking the money.
scene 8
looser comes into a restaurrant and orders coffee and he removes his laptop from his bag and starts checking about the vintage camera on internet
he removes lays wafers and starts eating. [close up shot of the lips, eyes and the laptop.]
suddenly the a friend enters and snatches the wafers pack and say. what are you eating.
looser : give me that.
friend 3 : you this, [throws the wafer down on the floor] eat this like a dog. thats what who are for us. what are you watching on laptop.
losser shuts the laptop : thats no of your business.
friend 3 : whats thats a camera from another dimension. come here babe, let me show you someone.
looser looks down.
friend 3 to his girl : look this crap thinks he is one of us, he is doing photography so he thinks he can hangout with rich people. you dont belong here boy. this place is for people like us, look at my girl. have you ever been with a girl like this or ever had a girlfriend in your life. [the girl is also laughing] now take that cam and take a picture and by watching the picture, you can only dream of becoming like me.
looser looks at them smiles and takes the picture
the end

CHAPTER FOUR

written by : yogendra nikale.
tittle : lockdown.
ratan wakes up in his room and wacthes around. the alcohol bottles were empty.
ratan goes out and buys alcohol.
smokes o the street shot.
people watching on phone and television news of covid.
ratan entering house and drinking and mom bringing him food.
his parents watching news on the tv. about covid.
ratan drinking and watching movies on his phone. ratan gets a message of covid. he avoids it.
in news the covid in china. and it may spread.
ratan going in wine shop and buying alcohol again.
ratan drinking with kaalia.
kaalia : bhai daru khatamm hogayela hai.
ratan removes money from his pocket.
ratah : lena. manga aur. tu apna dost hai. tere liye jaan bhi hajir hai.
they both drinking.
covid has spreading world wide news.
ratan eating food at home. and yelling his mother. i dont eat such food. tigers only eat meat.
in news people watching first case n kerala.
raatan walking out for alcohol an watching everyone

wearing mask. and laughs at them saying "you pussy's"
ratan buying alcohol.
the wine shop guy telling the wineshops will be closed take some more.
ratan : dont worry, our government will take care of everything. the vaccine will come in few days
ratan going home drinking. watching about corona. ratan laughs and changes his song and plays on you tube piley piley piley.
on news modi announces about the lockdown 23rd march. and ratan is sleeping.
next day ratan wakes up.
ratan asks for money to his mother.
mother : kuthe challa,
ratan : baher daru anaila.
mother : arey ratan, baher sarva band ahe.
ratan : nai aplyala bheten kuthe pan.
mother : thamb nako jau police martey sarvanna.
ratan : ka martin , mi kai crime kella kai.
mother : ek minta thamb.
mother to father : aho aikana, tumchya kade daru tummi anun thevli ahe. dya na thodi asli tar.
ratan watches at the stock of alcohol.
father : nai, mi ek themb nahi denar.
ratan : aai tu kashala magtey. ratan mhantat mala. mai gheun yeto. tu paise de.
ratan was going out and she stops him
mother : thamb bala. mask gheun jaa.
ratan : mask, bisk mi nahi ghalat. ye tum ghabarta ye corona firona la. mi nai ghabrat.
ratan goes out of the house.
mother watches him going and watches his father. and father is watching the news that people are getting beaten

up in the street.
ratan goes out and he finds no one. there was no on the street.
ratan watches a check post and goes there. and as he goes near he watches police beating and they watch him also. they start running after him.
ratan starts running and hides behind the house in a chawl and there comes people running from opposite direction. and police were after them.
the people passes by and one of the police watches ratan.
police : sahe ek bhetlai.
ratan comes out.
ratan : saheb mi atta just gharatun aloy. emergency ahe.
police : kai jhaley, kon azari ahe ka.
ratan : nahi saheb wineshop la challoy.
police from back hits on his back.
police : aighalya ith lokka martat ahe ani tu bina mask wineshop la chaallai.
they starts beating him.
ratan : saheb, saheb pan majhi chuki kai.
police : salya purya deshat curfue ahe ani tu baher firtoy.
they starts beating again. and ratan runs from there and they start running after him.
ratan hides in a rickshaw. and police runs in a different direction.
ratan : what the fuck is going on.
from the bak of rickshaw there comes a voice.
the stranger "corona chalra hai. "
ratan looks at the luggage spot a man was hidding.
ratan : tu kya karra hai.
starnger : arey mujhe turkey laga tha. daru lene aya tha. sab band hai.
ratan : arey bhai mein bhi, abhi kaha milegi.

starnger : abhi chalte hai ek addey pe. wahapar mila toh mila. par mehenga milega dost.
ratan : arey kitne ka bhi milne de. chalega. hai kidhar ye jaggha.
stranger and ratan goes at that spot in a steath mode. and hidding from police.
they both reach at the spot.
one guy was selling whiskey. in a slum
they both reach near him.
that guy brings them inside the chawl.
the whiskey selller : a bhai tera mask kidhar.
ratan : mein bhulgaya gharpe.
wiskey seller : bhai aisa mat kar. fas jayega. bol tujhe kya chahiye.
ratan : mujhe ek khamba de.
whiskey seller : 4 quater milegi, par 2 hazar lagenge bhai.
ratan : ek quater 500 rupye ko.
wwhiskey seller : bhai ye lockdown hai , agey jakar bohot mehenga honevala hai.
ratan : thik hai 2 quarter de dal.
ratan to stranger : tujhe bhi leneka hai na.
stranger : mere pass sirf 300 hai, 200 kam hai.
ratan : sorry yarr mere pass abhi kuch paisa nahi hai.
whiskey seller : toh desi le, 300 mein desi bechta hu mein.
starnger : chalega dedal [gives him the money]
whiskey seller : tum log idher hi rukho mein abhi jakar ke aya stock under rakha hai. sirf bahar open mein mat jaana.
ratan and the stranger waits outside
ratan : ye ayega na, kya paisa lekar udh jayega.
starnger : tension mat le mein dryday ko yaha se hi letta hu.
ratan : kya darring hai na bindass dhanda karra hai.
stranger : arey log police se bhi nahi darte.
and they hear sound of the whiskey guy yelling and police

beating him and bringing him from inside where the whiskey guy went to bring the alcohol.
ratan and starnger : aichya gavat.
and they both start running.
ratan : arey mera paisa hai uskey pass.
starnger : arey bhai mera bhi toh hai, apni jaan bacha aur bhag.
ratan and starnger stops at a spot.
ratan : abhi kya karenge. daru ka kya karu.
stranger : nikal ja apne gharpe. ye kharab time chalra hai.
starnger starts walking and and talking.
starnger : mein toh challa, kon bahar rukh ke police ka maar khayega.
suddenly the stranger gets hit on his shoulder. it was the police.
starnger shoults.
police starts beating him and few of them starts running after ratan .
ratan starts running. and knocks the home's of the people.
ratan : please let me in. police are after me.
the people : no we cannot. its risky.
somesay "you didnt even wear a mask. we cannot risk our family's life".
ratan runs and hides behind the gate and the police van passes by.
and ratan takes breath of releif.
ratan checks if he is having a handkercheif in his pocket. but there was no handkerchief. then he wipes his sweaty face with his tshirt. and he watches around there was a fallen mask on the street.
ratan to himself: i need a mask.
ratan goes back to his flashback and remembers his mother asked for a mask.

next ratan removes his underwear and wears it on his face face like a mask. and exits the compund and a guy from the balcony was making a video of him.and laughing.

cut to

sunset

ratan walking on the streets hidding from police.

ratan talking to himself " atta kala nusta kaaliach madat karu shakto"

ratann finds a guy in rickshaw with his uniform.

ratan walks near him and says " ohh sahab rikshaw chakegi kya."

rikshaw driver : arey kon jayega, bahar police ki maar khnaeke liye.

ratan : chalo na, mujhe mere dost ke ghar jaana bohot jaruri hai. tum jitna bole utne.

rikshaw driver : kuthe jayeche ahe.

ratan : nnavi mumbai.

rikshaw driver : arey navi mumbai bharpur lamb jhaley.

ratan : chala na please. mmajhi yevdi madat kara.

rikshaw driver : 3 hazar rupaye lagtin.

ratan repeats it : 3 hazar. he tar khup zhale.

rikshaw driver : yevdech lagtin, parvadtai tar chal. nahi tar dusri rikshaw shodh.

ratan watches him and remembers his mother bringing him mobile.

ratan throwing his mobile in flashback and saying yevda sasta tumhi vapra. udya chya udya mala note 10 pahije.

ratan : 3 hazar rupaye nahi ahe, pan ha mobile ahe chalen ka.

ratan gives him mobile and and the rickshawdriver watching him.

cut to

rickshaw shot of hand kick and the rick in running.

rickshaw driver in the running rickshaw. says"wear the white shirt from behing and i will tell police that you are a doctor on the checkpost.

ratan wears the white shirt and sits

they reach at kaalia's place. ratan askks him to stop.

ratan was getting out of the rickshaw. the riskshaw driver stops him and says "bhai shirt tar return de, mala ajun ek bhada bhetu shakto"

ratan removes the shirt and keeps it back. and gets out of the rickshaw.

ratan knocks at the kaalias house.

kaalia opens the gate and watches.

kaalia : who is it.

ratan removes his mask and says " its me"

kaalia : how did you do this, how did you traveled from there till here.

ratan : dont ask just open the door.

kaalia opens the gate and ratan enters.

kaalia was sitting outdoor drinking in his porch.

ratan : atleast someone with alcohol.

ratan starts making his pack.

kaalia : what are you doing.

ratan : pack banara hu.

kaalia : dekh bhai, abhi pack banaya hai toh pi dal. par isse jyada nahi milega.

ratan : aisa kya bolra hai re.

kaalia : sorry bhai, lockdown aur daru kidhar bhi nahi milegi.

ratan : ek khamba hai yaar tere pass. mein thodi piyunga toh kya hojayega.

kaalia : dekh bhai daru mein dosti nahi. baki tu kuch bhi mangle.

ratan keeps his pack down and starts leaving.

kaalia : kkidhar jaara hai, pack toh maar.
ratan : sorry yaar, yehi sunne ka tha mujhe.acha hua ye lockdown hua, tera asli roop dekhne ko mila mujhe. chal tu apna mood bana. aur mein apna safar teh karta hu.
cut to
ratan coming out with his underwear on his head and starts walking and stops near a jungle and sits down.
ratan watches a alcohol bottle with fried chicken on the street and he goes there.
ratan wonders who has kept this in the middle of a jungle.
ratan sits there and starts making his pack. and as he watches above there was a witch on the trees.
ratan gets up and starts running. and the witch flying and following him.
ratan watches a temple and enters it and gets inside and he starts praying lord help me lord.
and the witch couldnt enter the temple.
after watching the god he gets back in his flash back of his mother praying and ratan getting angry. telling "stop this smoke and this noice"
and coming out of the house and lighting the cigerete.
cut to
he sleeps there and watches the witch go.
cut to
in the morning ratan is sleeping and someone kicks him.
watchman of the temple "hey uth kya karra hai idhar chal nikal idhar se"
ratan gets up and watches him and starts walking.
ratan remebers his mom was sweeping the floor and cleaning his bottles and ratan gets up.
ratan : kai bekar bai ahe, kadhi neet jhopun nai deth.
cut to
ratan walking and watches few families walking on the

street.
ratan asks them where are you headed.
they reply : we are all finished, all our business is gone. we are headed walking towards our village.
ratan : why the transport.
people : they are asking for 5000 per ticket. we cannot afford that. so we have no other way. where are you headed.

ratan : no where, i have no where to go.
people : ok come with us. you can stay in our village.
ratan starts walking with them.
walking shots day and night.
they are giving him water and mask while travelling shot.
ratan watches police and people are giving food to the homeless and travellers.
ratan also gets a plate.
while eating ratan rmembers his mother he misbehaved.
one guy dies during the way.
people trying to help him.
cut to
ambulance comes and takes him away.
cut to
ratan walking and his sleeper is destroyed. and then he is walking barefoot.
cut to
ratan and people buying raw food and the shop keeper says its 100 bugs.
ratan : but the mrp says its 30.
the shopkeeper : ok go and buy.where you get it.
cut to
at night.
people coocking on the street and ratan is watching
cut to

ratan and people reached the village.
and people from the village made tents for them.
ratan : kitti divas rahayche ithe.
people : 15 days of quarntine. then we can live normally.
cut to
ratan working in the village farming and helping villagers.
one of the guy comes and says the shopkeepers from the cities are selling on tripple rates.
one farmer making a video dont do this, we are selling food very cheap from before, for poor. let them eat. you wont find a place in hell if make money now.
few months later. ratan all beared up.
ratan working in the farm and a guy comes running.
guy : ratan the government has removed the lockdown. people can travel now.
ratan : i think now its time to see my parents.
ratan getting shaved, says good bye to the villagers and then leaves.
cut to
ratan travelling in the bus towards his house.
cut to
knocking his house door and getting in.
after watching ratan his mother gets shocked and starts crying
ratan : yeah lockdown madhe mala lakshat ale, ke family le important ahe.
cut to
ratan drinking in his house and his mother says.
mother to father : ha 15 divas changla rahila ani vapas piyaychi chalu keli.
father : jaude ek na ek divshi tyachi daru band hoin.
mother : kai mahiti ha divas kadhi yenar ahe.
cut to

ratan wakes up and goes towards their parents for money.
ratann : paise kuthe thevle.
mother : tikde ahe paise, pan baher sarva band ahe.
ratan : ka.
mother : tv lav ani bagh.
ratan : switches on the tv and watches the second wave of covid.
ratan looks at the his father. his father was drinking.
ratan then looks at his fathers stcok of alcohol and he looks back at him his father laughs loudly hahahahahahaha.
the end.

CHAPTER FIVE

written by yogendra nikale
tittle : one ticket [shot song video]
song : little things [wanted]
office boy gets up on the alarm clock and he goes walking towards the office and he stops at lotery seller blind old man having a billboard saying one ticket can change your life. the boy reads it and goes to the office.
the security lets everyone pass without the id except him and he watches, and knows he is getting bullied.
in the office there is acolleage who always hits im on the head when he is working.
when ever he is in the bathroom a fat guy puts garbage from the above.
there is one hot chick, the boy was watching her and there comes the fat boss with the load of the files and shows him the watch.
everyone leaves the office except him. he works late due to load given to him.
as he exits the office there is a hot girl in mustang on the street on signal, they look each other and they both leave to their path.
and one smoker on the street always smokes on his face while passing by.
again next day the boy heads towards the office, he watches the man with the bill board saying im serious. the boy reads

it, ignores and heads towards the office.
again the same bully
next day he wakes up the blind man bill board says last chance. the boy buys the ticket and starts watching the result online .
he watches the hot girl from the office passes by and watches the resul all his ticket numbers matches except last 2 result about to come
he does his work side by side and again he watches the result last number result about to come
he goes to the toilet again the garbage bully by the fat guy.
he comes towards his desk clearing the garbage and he watches the result, that he had lost. he becomes very diisapointed and there comes a college and hits him on his head. in anger he takes the key board hits on his head.
he walks towards the garbage bin caries it and puts it on the fat guy and climbs the desk and jumps on the top of the bin.

then he watches the fat boss has come with some files he runs towards her and she drops the file and also starts running watching him mad. he grabs a file and roles while running and catches her and puts the file in her mouth
he watches the hot chick he goes near her starts kissing and while leaving the office he starts the fire alaram and everyone gets wet.
the boy comes near the security and takes the id card in his hand and slaps on his chick.
and as he comes out the smoker was passing he snatches his smoke from left hand and hits him with a right and as the smoker falls he kicks on his butt and smokes.
as he looks forward he watches the mustang girl. he takes the puff of a smoke jumps in the car kisses the girl and exhales the smoke. and the car goes. and the camera pans

on the old man with a bill board saying i told you so.
the end.

CHAPTER SIX

written by yogendra nikale
music video
song : still will kill

father yelling boxer at home

father : every time you are fighting [boxer with a black eye] seriously i dont want you in my house [neighbours are watching this conversation from the window] just get out

boxer : how will i survive.

father : find your own way, quite a fighter you are, go and fight and survive.

boxer : you want me out of this house, fine, i just had enough of this sheat.

the boxer gets anoyed and comes out of the house

boxer walks down the street and 3 ganbangers follow

under the bridge boxer and his 2 friends are smoking and drinking .

on the street a guy comes and walks towards the bridge and one friend has a laser light, to informing them someone is coming

as the guy goes under the bridge, 3 of them atack him and rob his money, watch and walet.

these guys are partying in club and having fun.

the guy who got mugged is in hospital.

they enter the street boxer club

everyone are putting bets on fighters .

after a match the boxer enters the ring and his friend puts a bet on him.
the fight starts and boxer wins and crowd cheers.
the boxer and his friends parties with girls in the club.
the guy who got robed enters the house and watches his face all smashed and punches on the mirror.
he goes over the bridge he watches boxer mugging a guy again.
boxer is again partying with friends on streets with grafiti on the wall.
boxer enters the cllub for a fight, he gives the money to bet.
as the fight was going on cop raids the place.
boxer some how manages to exit.
the guy who got mugged, he looks in the broken mirror and opens the closet and removes the gun.
the boxer checks his pocket, there is no money.
he walks toward the bridge and stops under the bridge.
there come the mugged guy with a gun and he is wearing a hood.
he comes passes by the boxer and boxer follows him.
the guy realizes boxer is following him he removes the gun and turns around.
he points the gun towards the boxer and removes his hood.
after removing the hood boxer recognizes the marks and comemore closer towards him .
the guy stares at him and lower down the gun. as he lowwer downs the gun boxer hops on him and fire shot.
the boxer walks away and guy is lying dead on the street.
the end.

CHAPTER SEVEN

written by yogendra nikal
music video script
song : we in here
cycle stunts.
skate board guy skating
parkour on the street and grafiti on the walls
bike stunts on the road.
the skate boardguy dashes the cop car, the cop comes out of the car and starts beating the kid
huge guy comes to stop the cop, the cop starts beating the huge guy as well and all the team watching him.
the cop puts his head on the car and keeps a stick on his neck. and everyone staring and watching this brutal act.
cop then leave with his car.
and everyone comes near the huge guy and and the huge sign im ok.
the cop is outside the police quarters and the kids are following him. and they contacting eachh other on radio.
the cop goes home the kids are following.
the cop in the mall the kids are following.
the cop then goes in a building apartment. and the kids are following.
as he enters the room . they contact on radio and the huge guy is on another building with binocular watching what happening in the room.

the cop is beating a woman and raping her.
next day a smart guy contacts that lady on the street. and the lady gives him the keys.
the kids are following him again.
and he goes in the building to trouble the lady again.
the cop had tied the lady on the bed and was beating her with a cane.
the huge guy enters the room and everyone are next to him.
the cop tries to reach the gun they catch him. and tie him on the bed and they beat him and video record it.
they tie him and put him in a bad and put him in a trunk and drop him on the hill.
the walk of everyone [cinematic scene]
the end.

Printed by Libri Plureos GmbH in Hamburg,
Germany